Starry, Starry Night

Adapted by Jordan D. Brown
Based on the screenplay
"Night of a Bazillion Stars"
written by Joe Purdy

Ready-to-Read

Simon Spotlight
New York   London   Toronto   Sydney   New Delhi

SIMON SPOTLIGHT

An imprint of Simon & Schuster Children's Publishing Division

1230 Avenue of the Americas, New York, New York 10020

This Simon Spotlight edition April 2019

© Copyright 2019 Jet Propulsion, LLC. Ready Jet Go! is a registered trademark of Jet Propulsion, LLC.

"Night of a Bazillion Stars" © 2018. Lyrics by Craig Bartlett and Jim Lang

SIMON SPOTLIGHT, READY-TO-READ, and colophon are registered trademarks of Simon & Schuster, Inc.

For information about special discounts for bulk purchases, please contact Simon & Schuster Special Sales
at 1-866-506-1949 or business@simonandschuster.com.

Manufactured in the United States of America 0319 LAK

2 4 6 8 10 9 7 5 3 1

ISBN 978-1-5344-3059-4 (hc)

ISBN 978-1-5344-3058-7 (pbk)

ISBN 978-1-5344-3060-0 (eBook)

Sean, Sydney, and Mindy
were staring at a strange object
in their backyard.
"Jet, what is that thing?"
Sean asked.

"It's a tent from Bortron 7," Jet answered.

He explained that on Bortron 7, his home planet, this tent is used for sleeping outside to look at the stars.

"You mean a backyard sleepover?" asked Sydney.

"Sleepover! What a great Earth word!" Jet said.

Later that day everyone returned
to the tent.
"I brought snacks, binoculars,
comic books, and my sleeping bag,"
Sydney said.
Jet laughed. "A bag to sleep in?
That is *so* Earth!"

"We can use your binoculars to count all the stars in the sky!" Mindy said.
"No one can count all of them, Mindy," said Sean.
"There are way too many."
"I'm going to try!" Mindy said. "Hey, why did you pack so much stuff?"

"My mom made me bring all these things," Sean explained. "I have flashlights, sunblock, and bugblock. My parents say you should always be prepared for every mission. Even a

Jet looked up at the sky and
smiled.
"I love the night! You can see so many
stars and planets," he said.

"And they all twinkle!" Mindy gushed.
"Wait, do all stars twinkle?" Sean asked.

"That's the big question!" Jet replied.

Just then Jet's parents,
Carrot and Celery, came outside.
"How's the over-sleep going, kids?"
Carrot asked.

"It's called a sleep-UNDER,"
Celery explained.
"It's actually called a *sleepover*."
Sydney corrected them.
"Ah, a sleepover!" Carrot said.
"Earth words!"

"All right, Earth friends,
it's time for a grand tour
of my tent from Bortron 7!"
Jet announced.
The friends walked inside
and looked around.

Jet unzipped the roof.
"The tent has a see-through roof so you can look at the moon, planets, and stars!"

Jet's parents entered the tent. "I made a sleepover snack called s'mores!" Celery said. Sydney said she loves s'mores— graham crackers, chocolate, and marshmallows.

But Celery's s'mores were made
of cake, barbeque sauce,
and cottage cheese.
They tasted a little different.
"Mindy! Time to come home!"
Mindy's mother called.

Mindy said she would look out her window at the stars and planets. "I'm going to give them all names and count them!" she said.

"We'll be looking up at the
stars and planets too,
Mindy!" Sydney told her.

"Sean, did you bring your birthday telescope?" Jet asked. Sean carefully took out his shiny, beautiful new telescope.
"Jet, please, please, please be extra careful with it," Sean pleaded.

Clang! Zong! Bong!

Sean looked over at Jet taking apart his telescope.

"Jet, look what you did!" Sydney cried.

"I'm sorry, Sean," Jet said.

Seconds later Jet had put
Sean's telescope back together . . .
sort of.
"Thanks. It's like new!
Wait, what is that?" Sean asked.
"Look!" Jet grinned. "Now it also
makes hot cocoa!"
Sean sighed. "I guess my telescope
will never be the same."
Glick! Zip! Zoom!
Jet's pet, Sunspot, fixed
Sean's telescope,
and it was really just like new.

After the telescope was fixed,
Sydney pointed it at the sky.
"I see two planets, Mars and
Venus!" she said.
"The stars twinkle, but the planets
don't," Sydney added.
"Let's find out why," Jet said.

He called up his friendly computer,
Face 9000.
"Greetings, everyone!" Face said.
"Here's the answer to your
big question."

Face explained, "Every star gives off light, but since stars are so far away from Earth, that light travels a very long distance. Light rays from stars bend in funny ways as they travel through space and through Earth's atmosphere."
(say: AT-mus-fere)
"So that's why stars look like they are twinkling! But what about planets?" Sydney asked.

"Planets are much closer to Earth,
so their light doesn't travel as far,"
Face said. "Therefore planets do not
look like they are twinkling."
Face said good night and disappeared.

Jet, Sydney, Sean, and Sunspot
lay on their backs and gazed
at the stars.
"*I've been to Venus and Neptune
and Mars,*

But the night sky there, well, *it hardly compares, to this fabulous view from this planet of ours*," Jet sang.

He smiled at his friends.

"I made that song up!" he said.

After Jet's song ended,
his mom called out, "Kids, bedtime!
Sleep tight, don't let the bacon bite!"
"I think it's 'don't let the bedbugs
bite,'" Sean said.

"Bacon, or bedbugs, or blueberries, as long as they don't bite!" Carrot said.

Jet grinned. "Best. Oversleep. Ever!"

In the distance they heard Mindy shout, "I counted three hundred million, one thousand, and seven stars. Good night!"

Read on to learn some more out-of-this-world facts and how to plan your very own over-sleep!

Our Solar System by the Numbers

- Our solar system is approximately 4.6 billion years old and 11.65 trillion miles long.
- Our solar system has 8 planets.
- Mercury and Venus have no moons, Earth has 1 moon, Mars has 2 moons, Jupiter has 79 moons, Saturn has 62 moons, Uranus has 27 moons, and Neptune has 14 moons. That's a total of 185 moons—and there could be even more we haven't discovered yet!
- Our sun is around 10,000 degrees Fahrenheit at the surface and around 27 million degrees Fahrenheit at the core.
- Our sun is approximately 109 times larger than Earth.

The closer a planet is to the sun, the faster it rotates around it. Here's what one year looks like on each planet based on its distance from the sun:

- 1 year on Mercury is equivalent to 88 days on Earth. Mercury is the closest planet to the sun.
- 1 year on Venus is equivalent to 225 days on Earth.
- 1 year on Mars is equivalent to 687 days on Earth.
- 1 year on Jupiter is equivalent to 4,333 days on Earth.
- 1 year on Saturn is equivalent to 10,759 days on Earth.
- 1 year on Uranus is equivalent to 30,687 days on Earth.
- 1 year on Neptune is equivalent to 60,190 days on Earth. Neptune is the farthest planet from the sun.

Life Cycle of a Star

Stars are born in great galactic nurseries called **nebulae** (a Latin word for "clouds"). As a star grows, it gathers gases and dust to become an infant star, called a **protostar**.

Once a protostar has gathered enough mass, it becomes a **main sequence star**. Our sun is currently a main sequence star. The bigger the star, the more light it will show, but this also means it has a shorter lifespan. But star lifespans are different from human lifespans. Every star has a lifespan of billions of years! So you don't have to worry about the sun burning out any time soon!

After burning for billions of years, eventually a star will start to die. First it becomes a **red giant**—a bright red star that gets hotter and hotter until it completely burns out.

Sometimes large main sequence stars die in a massive explosion called a **supernova**. A supernova creates a brilliant flash of light that equals the amount of light of an entire galaxy of stars!

Stargazing Tips

- The sky is always clearer in winter so be sure to plan your stargazing adventure in early winter and pack extra blankets!
- Bring a red flashlight to navigate at night. This will help your eyes adjust when looking at the stars! (The light in the flashlight needs to be red. Just putting red plastic over the light will not work.)
- Start with binoculars and bring a star chart to track and find your favorite stars!
- Be mindful of your surroundings and never go out to stargaze without a responsible adult!

If you're planning your very own over-sleep, here's a checklist for essential things to bring:

- Tent with tarp
- Sleeping bags, pillows, blankets
- Headlamps or flashlights (with extra batteries)
- Water and snacks (Remember to keep snacks in the car or away from your tent so park critters can't get to them!)
- Proper clothing for daytime, sleepwear, rainwear, extra comfy shoes
- Tent repair and first-aid safety kit—just in case!

Take Five!

Here are five fun questions for you about the story you've just read.

1. What did you learn today about stars and planets?
2. Where would you like to have a sleepover?
3. If you had a sleepover at a friend's house, what would you bring?
4. Where would you like to stargaze at night?
5. Which do you like better—stars or planets? Why?

When you have your sleepover, you and your friends can name your own stars!